I would like to dedicate this book to my amazing parents, Jim and Joan Wagner, who taught me to view mistakes and challenges as opportunities for growth and creativity. Also, this book is for my grandkids. This world needs great problem solvers...this world needs you!

Thank you to Keith, Josh, Joy, Sean and the rest of my family. I would also like to thank the many friends who have been by my side throughout this process, and of course, every student who walked into my classroom throughout my career. Your wisdom, support, patience, advice, trust, and love mean more to me than you will ever know!

~Terri

This incredible journey has taken my twins, Meryl and Liam from toddlers to teenagers. I hope to give them a fraction of the insights they have given me. I dedicate this book to my two favorite people.

~ Heather

Dear Reader:

This book has been more than a ten-year journey for me and Heather. We are both parents and educators. The idea for this story came from many years of learning from mentors, reading books, attending conferences, and valuable lessons of trial and error, both in the classroom and in our homes. We believe that children need to be taught how to solve problems, rather than be told how to solve them or to have problems always solved for them. We have seen through our experiences that when children learn to solve their own problems, they become more confident learners and leaders. "What Will You Do Missy Moo?" was written with the intent of generating conversations between adults and children in order to guide children to solve their own problems and to evaluate the consequences of their choices. Our hope is that while enjoying this story together, you will be able to use this problem-solving model in real-life situations, and that your child, or students, can make connections to their own day to day situations or conflicts they face.

As you read this story, you will notice that there are both good and not-so-good solutions given for every problem that our little cow, Missy Moo, encounters. We did this intentionally in order to help children differentiate between the two. The key is to take the child all the way through the process (when they are calm) by asking them how each solution might work. For example, when Missy Moo has a problem with the rooster, her mother gives her the option of kicking the rooster over the fence. We certainly do not promote using physical aggression as a solution to any problem. However, the teachable moments that come from offering choices like this allow your child or student to internalize the situation and brainstorm appropriate solutions. Children are amazing thinkers, and they want to do the right thing. In the back of this book, you will find some tips to help you make the most out of this story. Thank you for reading "What Will You Do Missy Moo?" and sharing it with your child or class. We hope you enjoy it!

Terri & Heather

WHAT WILL YOU DO, MISSY MOO?

Author:
Terri Turner

Illustrator:
Heather Welsh

"Mama Moo!" shouted the little calf named Missy Moo,
as she ran to her mother.
"Yes?" answered Mama Moo gently.
"Rooster crowed in my ear!"
"Oh no," said Mama Moo, "What will you do Missy Moo?"

"I don't know" cried Missy Moo.

"Hey, I know!" shouted Mama Moo (so Missy could hear with her aching ear). "You could go over and 'Mooooooooo' in Rooster's ear. What would happen then?"

Missy looked at her mama with great surprise. That sure would teach Rooster a lesson!

"I have another idea!" yelled Mama Moo.
"What is it?" Missy Moo asked curiously.
"You could kick that ol' rooster clear over the fence.
What would happen then?"

Missy pondered her mama's suggestion. She was a very
strong kicker, but her mama and daddy always told her to
kick only if she had a good reason.
"Hmmmm... is this a good reason?" Missy wondered.

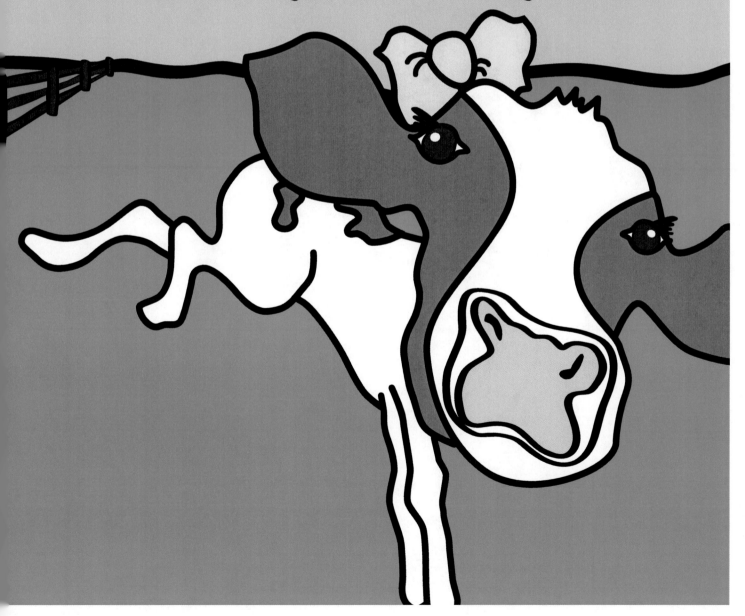

"I'm not sure what to do," said Missy as she shook her tail sadly. "Well, I have one more idea if you'd like to hear it," answered Mama Moo. Missy tried not to cry as she nodded her head. "You could always wear headphones when Rooster is around. What would happen then?"

Missy's eyes brightened.
She liked that idea,
but wasn't sure if it
would work...

What do

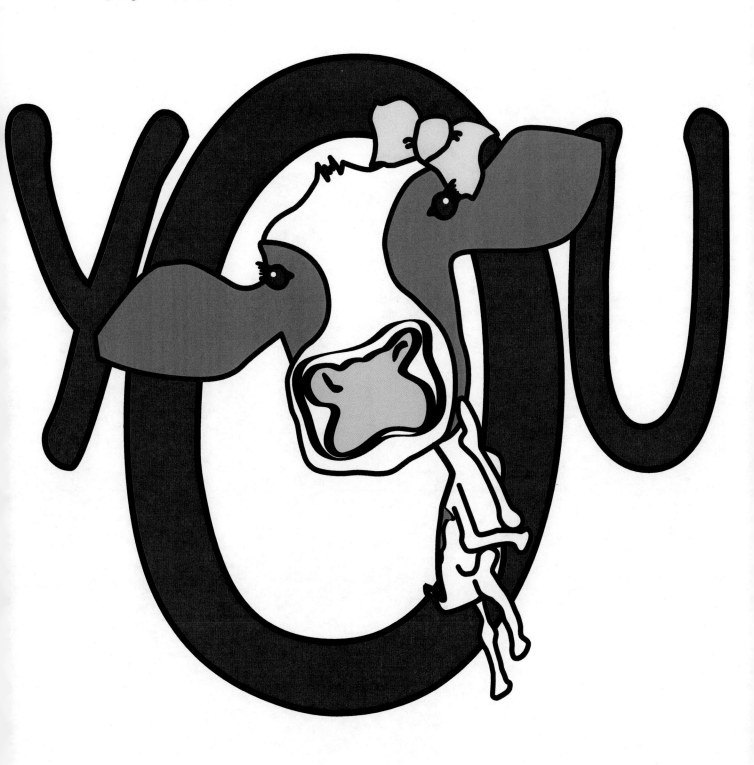

think Missy should do?

The next day, Missy trotted up
to Mama Moo, who was taking a nap
among the rich, green clover. "Mamaaaa!" mooed
Missy Moo. "What is it dear?" yawned Mama Moo.
"Horse told me that she can run faster than me,
because I run like a turtle!"

"Oh goodness" said Mama
Moo, "You must feel awful."
"I sure do," answered Missy, as she
sank down in the clover next to her mother.

Mama Moo licked her little calf and asked, "What will you do Missy Moo?"

Missy stared at her mother with her big, brown eyes. She had no idea what she could do. "Would you like to hear some ideas?" said her mother softly.

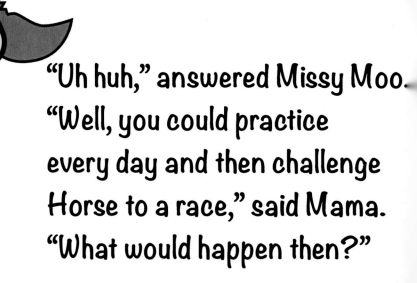

"Uh huh," answered Missy Moo. "Well, you could practice every day and then challenge Horse to a race," said Mama. "What would happen then?"

Missy Moo closed her eyes and imagined herself running across the finish line, leaving Horse in the dust. That would be cool, but would take a lot of work... and what if she lost?

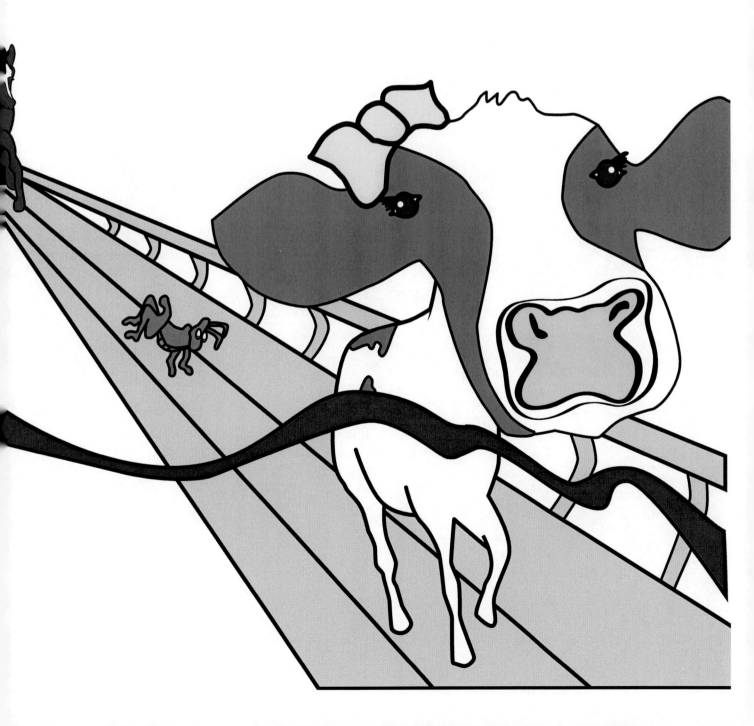

"Would you like another idea?" asked her mother.

"Sure," sighed Missy.

"Okay. You could tell Horse that her ears are too pointy and her tail is too bushy.

What would happen then?"

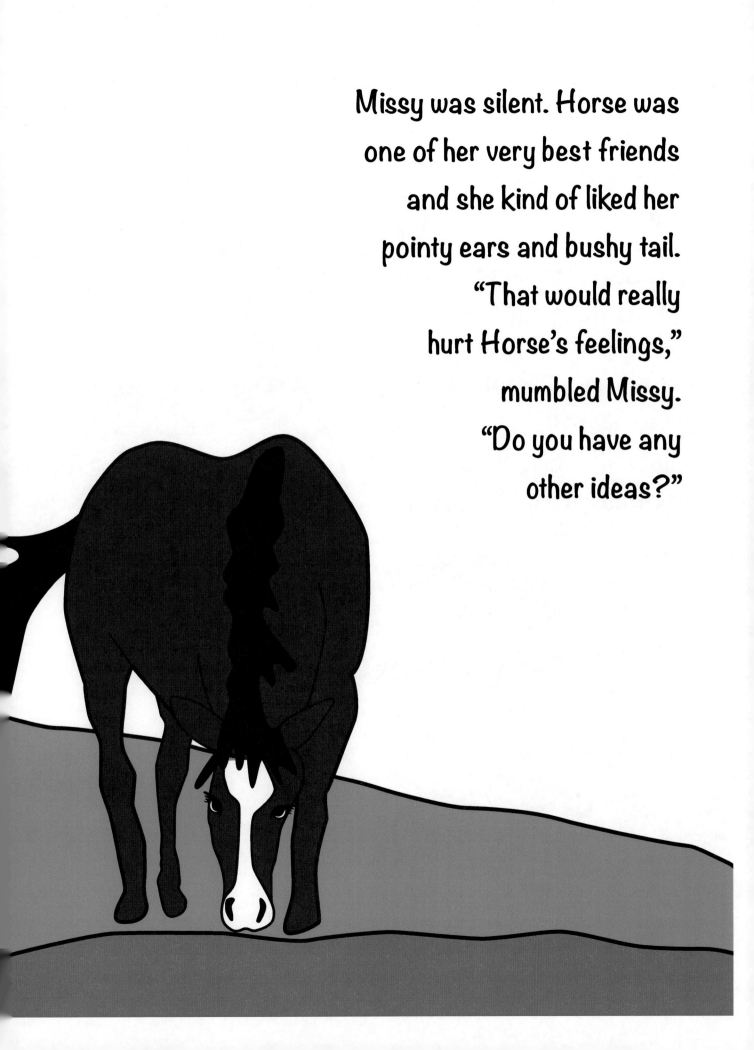

Missy was silent. Horse was one of her very best friends and she kind of liked her pointy ears and bushy tail. "That would really hurt Horse's feelings," mumbled Missy. "Do you have any other ideas?"

"As a matter of fact, I do. After this, I'm plum out," answered Mama Moo as she swatted a fly with her tail.

"You could remember all of the things you are good at, and not worry about what Horse says. What would happen then?"
"Maybe that would work," answered Missy Moo, but she wasn't exactly sure.

What do

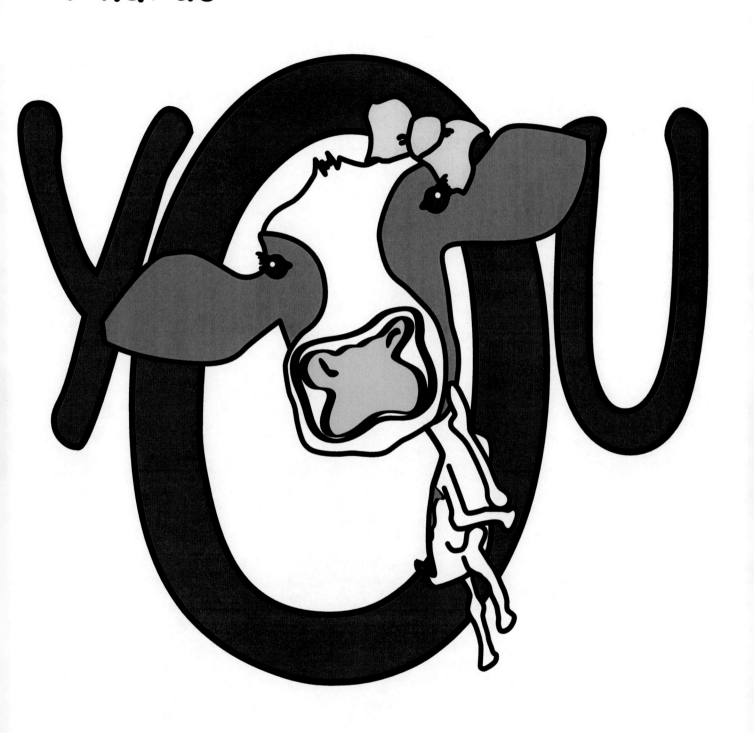

think Missy should do?

The morning sun rose over the pasture as Missy stood up and yawned. "Ready for school?" asked her father. "SCHOOL? Oh no!" cried Missy. "I forgot to do my homework!"

"Yikes!" exclaimed Papa Moo. "What will you do, Missy Moo?"

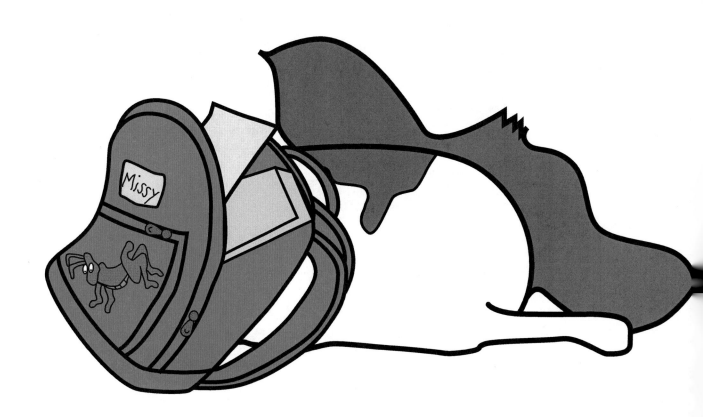

"I'm not sure. Maybe I should ask mom," whispered Missy. "Hmmmm, you could do that," answered Papa as he started to walk away.

"Unless you have some ideas," said Missy quietly.
Papa Moo stopped and swooshed his long black tail.

"Well, as a matter of fact, I might have a couple of ideas for you. You could skip breakfast and do your homework now. What would happen then?"

Missy tried to think, but the rumbling in her tummy was too loud. "Got any others?" she asked hopefully.

"Why, yes I do," said Papa Moo proudly. "You could just not do your homework. What would happen then?"

Missy was stunned. She couldn't believe what she was hearing! "No way! I'd have to miss my recess," she shouted. "Well, that would just be horrible," agreed Papa Moo.

"Wait! I have an idea," cheered Missy.

"Huh?" answered Papa.
"Huh?" answered Mama (who had been listening nearby).
"If I hurry and eat breakfast, and don't play with my
friends, I think I can get my homework finished."

"Wow!" whispered Papa Moo.

"Wow!" whispered Mama Moo.

"Thanks," smiled Missy Moo, as
she trotted off to eat her breakfast.

Before Reading

We have broken the story into sections with stopping points for conversation and problem-solving. Discuss what is happening in the pictures on each page before reading the words.   Encourage your child or students to make predictions about the story by asking the questions below, or make up your own.

- Who is Missy Moo?
- Where does she live?
- What other characters are in the story?
- What do you think this story will be about?
- What problems do you think Missy Moo may have?
- How do you think this story will end?

What do

think Missy should do?

During Reading

As with any story, the underlying purpose is always to model fluent reading, and foster a love for reading with your child or students. Make this story "come to life!" Give the characters different voices, read with expression, and have fun! We have strategically placed a grasshopper on each page for your child or students to discover and describe its location. See if they can spot him without any prompting from you.

- While reading with your child or students, have them check their predictions they made before reading. Example: "You predicted Missy Moo was going to cry when the rooster crowed in her ear. Were you right?"

- Throughout the story, Missy Moo encounters three different problems. Her mother and father each offer her various solutions. As you read these suggestions out loud, pause and ask your child or students if they think it is a good idea. Why or why not?

- After the first two problems, there are natural stopping points to help you discuss the possible choices (What do you think Missy Moo should do?) Ask your child or students to share other ideas about how Missy Moo can solve the problem. Have them explain why they think their solution would work.

- At the end of the story, the pattern of the text changes. This time, Missy Moo comes up with her own solution. Ask your child or students what they think of Missy Moo's solution. What would they do?

- Missy Moo is one confident little calf at the end of the story! Ask your child or students what they notice about how Missy Moo feels at the end of the story compared to how she was feeling at the beginning of the story.

After Reading

Did you know that re-reading books multiple times with children helps them to become better readers? When children hear stories over and over, they gain a better understanding, not only of the story, but what it sounds like to be a fluent reader. We hope that you and your child or students enjoyed this story, and that you will revisit it from time to time.

- Ask your child what their favorite part of the story was and why. What surprised them?

- If applicable, help your child or students make connections to Missy Moo's problems. For example, when Horse makes fun of how Missy Moo runs, you might say, "Wow! Missy Moo's feelings are really hurt. Has anyone ever hurt your feelings? How did that make you feel? What did you do? What could you do if that happens again?"

- Use the problem solving model with your child in every-day situations, while giving them a range of ideas. Be sure to always ask your child what would happen if they made that choice. Doing so helps them to think about the consequences of their choices.

- Let your child and students see and hear you solving your own day to day dilemmas. Make sure they are concrete and age-appropriate. For example, "I can't find my phone! Let's see...I can sit here and cry but that's not going to help me. I can go buy another phone, but that is pretty expensive! I can ask everyone to help me look for it, and maybe they can help me find it. I think I'll ask for help."

- When you see your child or student using problem solving skills, let them know that you've noticed how independent they are becoming!

When Opportunity Comes Knocking...

Here are some examples of "teachable moments" that may arise. Remember to model respect by having one-on-one conversations and not in front of others. It is always important to make sure that whatever the situation, all parties are calm. Think about the times when you have been upset...how easy is it for you to come up with a solution to a problem?

In the classroom:

- **Tattling**: "He called me a name." "She took my eraser." If you are a teacher, tattling just seems to come with the territory, on a daily basis! Asking kids what they can do, and giving them options is going to decrease the time you spend listening to tattling...yay!

- **Lost Items:** You just finished your lesson and have sent the kids off for independent work. You see one of your students sitting at their desk staring blankly into space. You go over to them and ask why they're not doing their work. "I can't find my pencil," comes the reply. The easiest and fastest way to approach this problem is to just give them another pencil. However, if you choose to do this, you will be giving them a pencil pretty much every day of the school year, and do you really want to do that? I (Terri) have seen kids be incredibly creative with this one. A few have resorted to finding a piece of pencil lead on the floor or in their shared caddy at the table. It certainly wouldn't have been my choice, but it worked and the problem got solved without me having to give them a new pencil.

- **Friendship Problems**: Name calling, hurt feelings, being left out, etc., can interrupt learning and sometimes, change the whole climate of your classroom in just a matter of minutes. A great time to address these issues and have private conversations with kids is when the others are working independently, before/after school, during lunch...kids love having lunch with their teacher! The important thing to remember is that as a teacher, you are not only helping students learn to solve their problems independently, you are building strong relationships with your students, which will help to make your school year an enjoyable one!

At home:

- **Broken Toys:** Your screaming child comes running in holding their cherished toy that just got broken. First, you will need to help them calm down – effective problem solving can't occur when the brain is in an emotional state. This is a great time to model breathing, and will help you stay calm as well. When your child is calm, help them focus on what to do next, instead of dwelling on what happened. As a parent, it is super easy to jump to lecturing – "See? I've told you a million times to put your toys away and now, look what happened!" As tempting as this is, put yourself in your child's place: how willing are you to solve a problem when someone is telling you how badly you messed up?

- **Fighting With a Sibling:** There are lots of ways to handle this one, and it completely depends on the situation and each individual child. Ask yourself these questions before trying the problem-solving method: Do I have time for both kids to calm down? Can they solve the problem together, or will it just lead to more arguing? If one is clearly at fault, it might be best to problem solve with them first, then work with the other one regarding forgiveness.

- **Frustration:** Homework, learning to ride a bike, trying to tie shoes...and the list goes on. Kids get frustrated, and as a parent, it can sometimes break your heart. How awesome would it be if you could help take their frustration away? As stated before, it is never a good time to go through the problem-solving process when your child (or you) is in an emotional state. Timing is everything, and many problems do not need to be solved instantly. Find a time when both you and your child are calm and have time to talk. You may want to open the conversation with "I've noticed that you get really frustrated with _____. Would you like some ideas?"

Made in the USA
Las Vegas, NV
28 April 2021